For Piet
who told it

NO MOUSE FOR ME

An Easy-Read Story Book

written and illustrated by
ROBERT QUACKENBUSH

A GROLIER COMPANY

Franklin Watts
New York/London/Toronto/Sydney
1981

Library of Congress Cataloging in Publication Data

Quackenbush, Robert M
  No mouse for me!

  (An Easy-read story book)
  SUMMARY: Explains how a pet mouse could ruin
a house.
  [1. Mice—Fiction. 2. Pets—Fiction] I. Title.
PZ7.Q16No [E] 80-29529
ISBN O-531-03541-7
ISBN O-531-04303-7 (lib. bdg.)

R. L. 1.9 Spache Revised Formula

Here.

Take back your mouse.

I don't want it.

It would be *dangerous*

for me to keep it.

Because . . . .

A cat might come
and chase the mouse
I kept at my house.

Then a dog would come.

The dog would chase the cat.

The cat would chase the mouse.

See what would happen at my house!

Then a dogcatcher would come.

The dogcatcher would chase the dog.

The dog would chase the cat.

The cat would chase the mouse.

See what would happen at my house!

Then the dog's owner would come.

The dog's owner would chase the dogcatcher.

The dogcatcher would chase the dog.

The dog would chase the cat.

The cat would chase the mouse.

See what would happen at my house!

Then the riot squad would come.

The riot squad would chase the dog's owner.

The dog's owner would chase the dogcatcher.

The dogcatcher would chase the dog.

The dog would chase the cat.

The cat would chase the mouse.

See what would happen at my house!

Then a rescue team would come.

The rescue team would chase the riot squad.

The riot squad would chase the dog's owner.

The dog's owner would chase the dogcatcher.

The dogcatcher would chase the dog.

The dog would chase the cat.

The cat would chase the mouse.

See what would happen at my house!

Then the news reporters would come.

The reporters would chase the rescue team.

The rescue team would chase the riot squad.

The riot squad would chase the dog's owner.

The dog's owner would chase the dogcatcher.

The dogcatcher would chase the dog.

The dog would chase the cat.

The cat would chase the mouse.

See what would happen at my house!

Then the army and navy would come.

The army and navy would chase the reporters.

The reporters would chase the rescue team.

The rescue team would chase the riot squad.

The riot squad would chase the dog's owner.

The dog's owner would chase the dogcatcher.

The dogcatcher would chase the dog.

The dog would chase the cat.

The cat would chase the mouse.

See what would happen at my house!

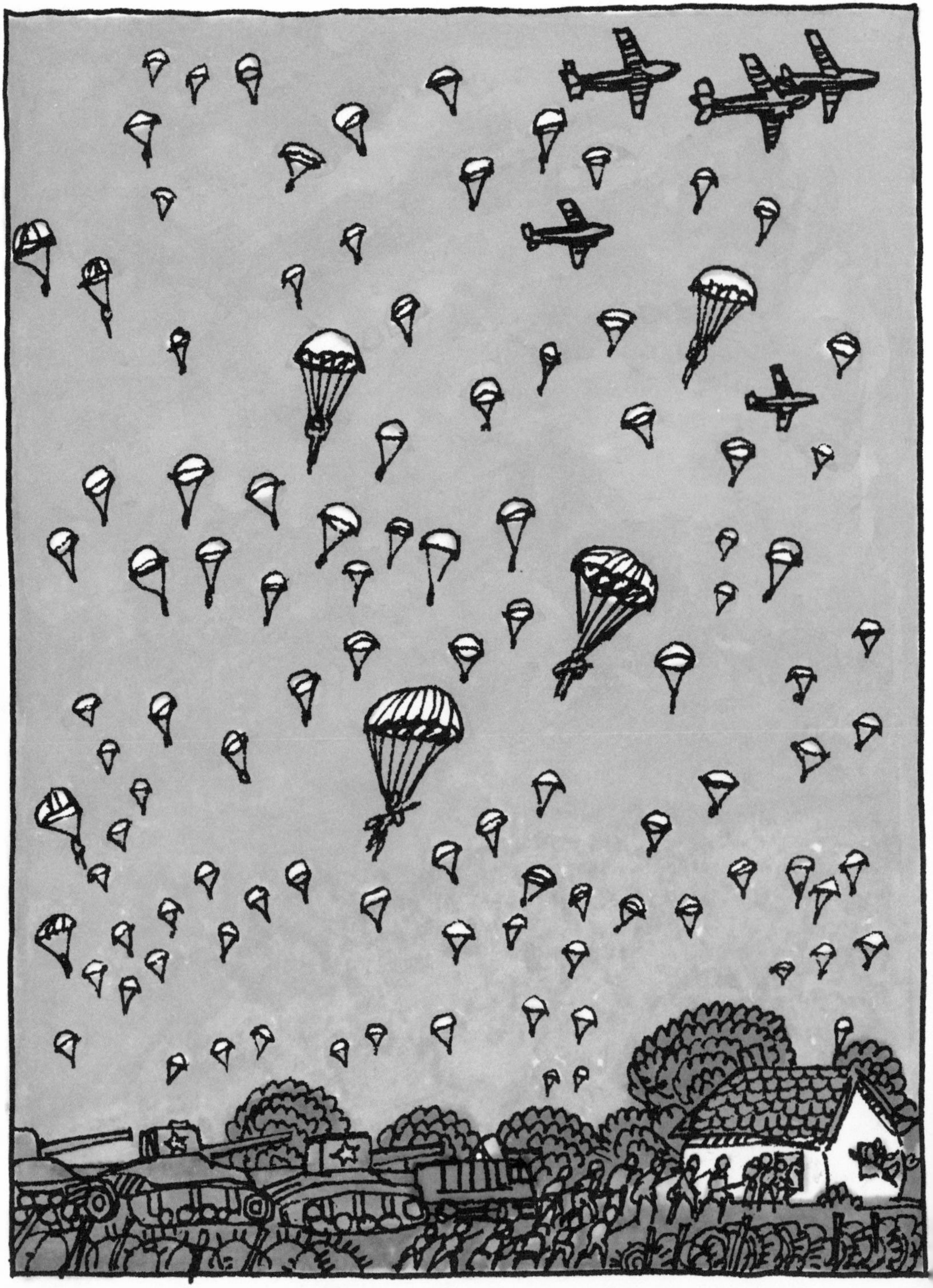

Then the air force would come.

The air force would chase the army and navy.

The army and navy would chase the reporters.

The reporters would chase the rescue team.

The rescue team would chase the riot squad.

The riot squad would chase the dog's owner.

The dog's owner would chase the dogcatcher.

The dogcatcher would chase the dog.

The dog would chase the cat.

The cat would chase the mouse.

See what would happen at my house!

TERRIBLE THINGS WOULD HAPPEN!

And all because of a little mouse.

So give me my money back.

I'd rather have a snake.